AF491224

# Serving the CEO: A Billionaire Surrogate Story

Juliana Raine-Ye

Published by Juliana Raine-Ye, 2021.

This is a work of fiction. Similarities to real people, places, or events are entirely coincidental.

SERVING THE CEO: A BILLIONAIRE SURROGATE STORY

**First edition. March 17, 2021.**

Copyright © 2021 Juliana Raine-Ye.

Written by Juliana Raine-Ye.

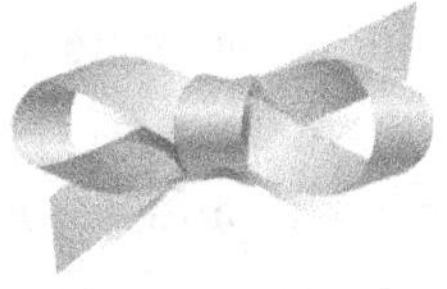

# Chapter 1



My fine arts degree was definitely not paying the bills, and my student loan payments were coming at me fast.

I was contacted by Mr. Hayes' current assistant, Mrs. Hann, through a recruiter. She wanted to meet with me almost immediately, and I jumped at the chance. I met with her in her office and even though I didn't have any relevant experience, Mrs. Hann seemed to be impressed by my answers.

After that first meeting, she told me she would set up a time for me to meet with Mr. Hayes privately.

If I can nail this interview and get the job then I could finally have some breathing room in my budget and start planning out my next career move. Maybe I could even use this position as a stepping stone to get into another industry.

I stepped out of the ornate elevator and waited. I was now in the penthouse suite of one of the most lavish hotels in South Florida. This was where Mr. Hayes had summoned me for an interview for the executive assistant position.

*Okay, I have to make a good impression. I can do this. I can do this. Just stay calm.*

After attempting to hype myself up, I looked around to see if anyone was coming to greet me.

*Should I just keep waiting?*

I decided to peek around the corner to check for any signs of life. Around the corner, there was a sitting room area with handsome but overstuffed armchairs and beyond that, I could see that there was a balcony with a view of the beach.

*Oh, this guy isn't just rich, he's wealthy.*

I suddenly started getting even more anxious. I had never been around this type of wealth before.

*God, I wish I was out on the water instead of here. I don't think I can do this-*

"How long were you planning on standing there?" I heard a husky voice say. I stepped around the corner into the sitting room and looked for the source.

Suddenly I realized there had been someone sitting in one of the chairs the entire time.

*Oh gosh, that must be Mr. Hayes.*

I begin to fidget with one of the pleats on my dress.

*What should I say?*

"Why don't you come and sit down?" Mr. Hayes says.

I gingerly stepped forward and made my way to an armchair across from the man, all while being aware of the sound of my flats click on the tiles with each step.

I lower myself into the seat slowly, look down at my shoes, and try to mentally prepare for the interview.

*Why am I so awkward?*

"Would you like something to drink?" Mr. Hayes says.

I look up from my shoes and notice he's no longer looking at me.

"No, thank you," I say quietly.

"Well good afternoon. I am Andrew Hayes, CEO of Hayes Healthcare Systems. I understand you are here to interview for the executive assistant position?" he continues, still not looking my way.

*Why do I find this so unnerving? I thought he would at least shake my hand. But he won't even look at me.*

"Yes, Mr. Hayes."

"Very good. Mrs. Hann told me all about you and your qualifications. She told me you were inexperienced yet intelligent, healthy, and have no romantic entanglements."

Hold on, what does my romantic life have to do with anything? And why would Mrs. Hann pass along that information?

"Mr. Hayes, I'm not sure what my personal life has to do with this executive assistant job..."

After a long pause, he finally looks my way and says, "Any executive assistant of mine will be expected to work long hours and really go the extra mile. I'm a very busy man - I do have a billion-dollar company to run. If you don't think you can be the hard-working, loyal assistant that I need because you have personal issues holding you back, then perhaps this isn't the position for you."

*Wait, how demanding could he really be?*

I'm nervous but also quite excited. Mr. Hayes definitely knows what he wants.

"I understand, Mr. Hayes."

"I don't think you do, Miss Lockmore. I want to be completely clear with you right now. If you took this job it would most likely ruin your life. You wouldn't have time to have much of a personal life. If you take this job I will be asking you to do some incredibly uncomfortable things."

*Do I really want this?*

I can feel my face getting hot. I don't really know what I'm getting myself into, but I definitely want to see where this goes.

I broke the stare and looked down at my shoes again. "I do understand the requirements of the position, Mr. Hayes. I don't have anything in my personal life that would get in the way of serving you. All I need is one chance to show you I can handle this."

*God, I hope I can do this.*

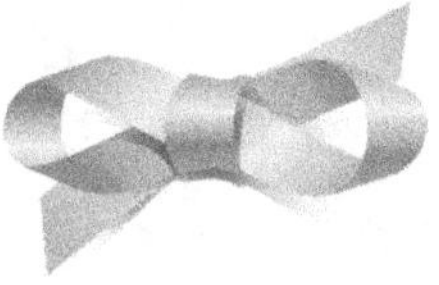

# Chapter 2

Andrew

Mrs. Hann told me that Sophie Lockmore was pretty - that was definitely a disservice. Sophie is absolutely stunning.

The black dress she's wearing hugs her curves in all the right places, her face seems almost angelic with all the delicate features, and I'm certain that her hair is just long enough for me to grab a fistful.

Sophie should have turned down the position while she had the chance. I don't know how I'll be able to get anything done with her around.

This might be the best thing Mrs. Hann has ever done for me. Even her strawberry-and-cream-scented shampoo is alluring.

I lean forward and extend my hand to Miss Lockmore. She reaches a hand out slowly and as soon as her fingers graze mine I can feel the electricity between us. I pull my hand away and look away from her.

*This is going to be more difficult than I thought.*

I look back at Sophie and see she seems just as surprised as I am.

*What is happening? I can't remember the last time I felt that with someone... Have I ever felt that way with someone? I have to have her. Let's see how serious she is.*

"I want you right now, Sophie."

*Your move, Miss Lockmore.*

# Chapter 3

S ophie

*What did he just say? He wants...me? Andrew Hayes wants me? As in, sex?*

*Maybe this is some sort of joke or test? He just wants to see how serious I am about the job.*

*I definitely need this job, but did I really hear him right?*

"I'm sorry, what?" I ask.

He begins to smirk at me. A very sexy smirk that makes my face feel hot and my mind go blank, but still a smirk.

*Why the heck is he smirking at me? What's so funny!*

"Let me rephrase. I want to fuck you right now, Sophie Lockmore."

*Okay yeah, I heard correctly the first time then.*

"Then we can discuss your start date," he adds.

*This can't be happening! Mr. Hayes is incredibly sexy and rich, but shouldn't we try to keep things professional? He's my boss! MY BOSS!*

*But I have the feeling he's not the type of person that takes no for an answer. And I did say I wanted to prove myself.*

While I think about the pros and cons of having sex with my future boss, I realize that I may or may not be but definitely am wet.

*Focus Sophie.*

"Was this even a legitimate interview? Are you just going to fuck me and then dismiss me?"

*Wow did I really use the word "fuck"?*

"Miss Lockmore, this was a serious interview. But there's just something about you that I find intoxicating. I'm drawn to you. And I want to know how your tight, wet pussy would feel wrapped around my cock."

*Oh, is that all? Gosh what is happening!*

*Okay, yeah, my panties are definitely soaked.*

I've never felt this way. In my last (only) relationship I don't think I was ever really aroused, we never even had sex. Jacob was fine with a half-hearted blowjob and he never had any interest in going near my pussy. It was only about him.

"You can have me, Mr. Hayes."

*Who am I?!*

His smirk turns into a wide smile and I can feel myself melting. Mr. Hayes gets up from the armchair and slowly walks towards me. He extends his hand and I take it and stand up. He begins leading me to another room.

We enter a room that looks like an office and he leads me to the large desk. He bends me over the edge so my cheek is on the desk, and I can feel myself getting wetter with anticipation.

*Oh! I didn't know I was into this.*

I feel his hand pull up the hem of my dress. Once the hem is above my waist I feel him start to rip down my panties roughly. He pulls them to around my ankles and then slips them off of both feet.

He then wedges a knee between my legs and pushes them apart. I hear the *zip* of his zipper and some shuffling.

I now feel his large cock rubbing against my damp pussy.

*I need him. Now.*

He puts one hand on my hip and then begins to place his tip at my entrance.

"Are you sure you want this, Sophie?"

*Of course I want this. I need this.*

I start to feel one of his hands gather my hair and tug, pulling my head off the desk.

"Sophie do you want this?" he whispers in my ear.

"Yes, Mr. Hayes."

I feel him quickly thrust his entire length into me and then stop. The fullness is intense and slightly painful. I let out a gasp and writhe slightly to get used to the feeling.

"Tell me when you want me to continue," he says with a firm grasp still on my hair.

"Continue," I croak.

"I need more than that, Miss Lockmore. Tell me how badly you wish to be fucked."

I feel my legs get weak. *Why is he doing this to me!*

I start to pant and I can feel my pussy tightening around him. *I need him. I need him. I need him.*

"Fuck me, please! I need you!" I manage to scream.

He responds by quickly thrusting in and out of me. He loosens his grip on my hair and grabs onto my hips to steady me.

I put my head back down on the desk, trying to get used to the feeling of being fucked - taking in every sensation. The feeling of his balls slapping against me, my hips slamming against the desk with each powerful thrust, and cycling between that new feeling of fullness and a feeling of emptiness.

As I get used to the sensations my body begins to take over. I can feel my hips thrusting back.

*I came here for a job and now I'm losing my virginity to my boss! I can't believe this is happening.*

I feel his breath tickle my neck as his thrusts begin to slow down.

"Miss Lockmore, are you fertile right now?" he growls.

*Fertile? Why does he care?*

"I don't just need a replacement for my current executive assistant, I also need an heir," he says.

*An heir? From me?*

At this moment I would love nothing more than to be impregnated by Mr. Hayes.

"I'm fertile," I say quietly.

"Good. Now, I want you to come," he whispers in my ear as his thrusts pick up speed.

*Come? Now? I can't do that on command. I can barely come on my own!*

As if sensing my hesitation I feel his hand reach between my legs, his fingers searching. I feel one of his fingers graze my clit and I moan.

*Oh gosh, I hope no one else is here in this penthouse.*

"Sophie, you need to come. I won't ask again," he growls, thrusting harder into me.

The combination of him touching my clit, the feeling of his cock stretching my pussy, and his husky voice in my ear is just too much. I feel the sensation inside of me climb higher and higher until it spills over the edge. I close my eyes and let it wash over me.

My pussy tightens with the climax and I feel his warm cum fill my pussy as he grunts.

"Good girl," he says as he slowly pulls out and I hear him zip up his pants.

I look behind me and I see him pull a handkerchief from his jacket pocket and wipe my inner thighs and pussy. I shudder as I feel the fabric against my sensitive pussy.

He pulls down the hem of my dress gently and then peels me away from the desk and helps me stand up straight.

I'm surprised by how gentle he can be as he smooths down my hair.

*I'd like to see more of him like this. This gentle side.*

He reaches down, picks up my panties, and places them into my hand.

"You can start Monday, Miss Lockmore," he says with a smirk.

*I can't believe I fucked my boss!*

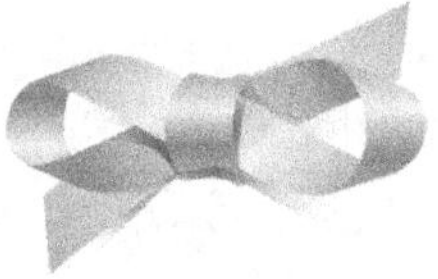

# Chapter 4

Andrew

Working with Miss Lockmore has been surprisingly wonderful. She's never late, pays attention to every detail, and she's even come up with a few ways to help streamline some processes.

I haven't fucked her since the interview, but that doesn't mean I haven't been thinking of her.

Almost every day I think of different ways I can have her. On the desk again, perhaps by the pool, maybe in one of the conference rooms after a staff meeting.

I've been waiting to fuck Miss Lockmore until she tells me that she's fertile again, but she hasn't mentioned anything.

*Maybe she's not interested in that part of the assistant position.*

As a reward for her hard work, I've decided to let Miss Lockmore accompany me on my next business trip.

We're on our way to the meeting and as usual, she's being incredibly professional. She's gone over the talking points twice, filled me in on the schedule for the rest of the day, and already placed our dinner order for later tonight.

I can't help but notice how sexy she looks. This time her hair is pulled back in a low ponytail and she's wearing a white blouse and some plum-colored pants. As she leans over her paperwork I can see her cleavage.

She tries to maintain her professionalism, but I know she'd still submit to me if I asked.

*I could fuck her right here in this limo. I could pull her over to me now, slowly unbutton her pants, pull down her pants and panties, and tell her to ride me right here and I know she'd do it.*

*God, she's so intoxicating.*

*I need to send Mrs. Hann the most lavish gift I can think of. I don't think I could have picked a better replacement.*

I usually just fuck once and then disappear, but something about Miss Lockmore is different.

*Maybe I want to do more than just fuck her.*

I can barely contain my composure.

"Thank you for getting everything organized for this trip," I say, trying to break the silence and get my mind off of burying my cock deep into her tight pussy.

"Oh, you're very welcome. I appreciate you inviting me on this trip," she responds without looking up from her papers.

I think I see her cheeks turn red.

We eventually arrive at the meeting place - a hospital billing company I've recently purchased. She gets out of the car slowly and I watch her walk towards the entrance.

*Maybe I could have a future with her? Be a normal family one day?*

*Yeah, I don't want to just fuck her.*

*Shit.*

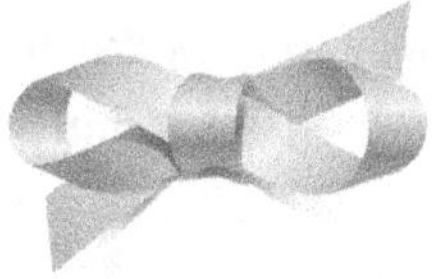

# Chapter 5

Sophie

"Thank you for all of your hard work, Miss Lockmore, I couldn't have done it without you," he says as we walk into the hotel suite.

*Why is he thanking me? He's the one that did all the work! I couldn't believe how easily he took charge in the meeting. He made it seem so effortless.*

"No need to thank me," I say quietly.

Working for Mr. Hayes has been a dream, I've learned so much from him and I feel like I'm starting to actually enjoy the industry and I can see myself doing this long-term.

I try to stay focused on my work, but my mind still wanders to that day. Feeling him inside of me, him filling me with his seed.

But he hasn't brought it up since, so I've tried to just get my mind away from any more thoughts of fucking or making love with him.

*Maybe he didn't enjoy it? Maybe he no longer wanted to make a child with me?*

"Dinner will be arriving soon, correct?" he asks, interrupting my thoughts.

"Yes, steak for you, and the tofu for me," I say, reminding him of our orders.

We both make our way to the table in the suite and sit down. The food arrives quickly and I eat quietly, looking at my plate the entire time.

"Did you not enjoy what we did after the interview?" he asks.

*What the hell? He can't just ask me that out of nowhere!*

I look up and him and he's staring at me, his brow furrowed slightly.

*He really wants an answer...*

*What do I say? Of course I enjoyed it, but he never mentioned anything related to what we did. I thought it was an off-limits topic.*

"I did enjoy it. I just was nervous about bringing it up. And I don't really know what to say about it," I answer honestly.

"Would you like to do it again?"

"Yes, I would."

"I've been wanting you every day since the interview," he says without blinking.

*He's been wanting me? Really? Does he actually want me or is this just about the heir?*

*I don't care, I want him, too.*

I stand up and make my way around the table towards him. I begin to unbutton my pants and I pull them down quickly, leaving my panties on. I step out of my shoes and then I start to unbutton my shirt but stop about halfway. This is all I have the nerve to do.

*Hopefully, he gets the message.*

He stares at me and places a hand on my hip, and rubs his thumb on my side.

*I don't just want to fuck him, I need more than that.*

"I want to taste you," I say, surprising myself.

He moves his chair back and begins unzipping his pants, he slowly takes out his cock and waits.

I kneel in front of him and take the tip into my mouth. His musk fills my nostrils and makes me more aroused. I slowly begin to work his shaft with my hands as I suck the tips.

I feel him grab a fistful of my hair and try to push my head down to force me to take more of him into my mouth. I push his hand away.

*I'm in control now.*

I try to take all of him into my mouth, I gag a little but I seem to manage it. I swirl my tongue around his tip and gently fondle his balls.

When I feel him start to tense up and I hear his breathing getting quicker, I stop sucking on him and look him in the eyes.

"I want you to come. I'm going to swallow your cum," I say boldly.

He touches my cheek and nods.

I take his tip into my mouth and I suck harder. Almost immediately he fills my mouth with his cum. When he's done with his spurts, I try to swallow it all, it tastes salty and sweet, and it's almost too much.

After swallowing his cum I take his tip into my mouth again and begin cleaning it off with my tongue. I hear him gasp and I feel him tense up again.

*I can't believe I'm making him this way!*

Once I'm finished I sit back on my heels and smile to myself.

*I just made him finish with my mouth! Yes!*

"Get on the bed and get on all fours, Miss Lockmore. And remove the rest of your clothes," he growls.

I stand up and pull down my panties, I then finish unbuttoning my shirt, I place it on the floor and I unsnap my bra and place it on top of my shirt.

I make my way to the bed and the boldness I was feeling before leaves my body.

*All fours? Right now?*

I try not to look at him as I get onto the bed and get into position. As I feel the cold air on my body I shiver.

Suddenly I feel his hands on my hips and he pulls me towards the edge of the bed. I then feel his fingers brush against my pussy and I moan.

His fingers begin rubbing my clit gently and I can feel myself getting wetter.

I start remembering our first time together. Mr. Hayes thrusting into me over and over. The feeling of his cum dripping from my fertile pussy.

*I need that again. I need him.*

"I need you, Mr. Hayes," I moan.

"You want to be fucked?" he asks.

*Fuck? Is that what I want? Not exactly... I need more than that.*

"I need you to make love to me," I say nervously.

I can feel him behind me placing his cock at my entrance and with a slow thrust he places himself all the way inside of me. Once he's all the way in, I feel his hands gently resting on my hips.

His thrust starts out slow and I savor each one. The feeling of being filled over and over makes my head spin.

As I'm enjoying his thrusts I remember something...

"Mr. Hayes, today is a fertile day."

His thrusts begin to pick up speed in response. I start to feel that familiar feeling of pleasure building deep inside of me.

As I feel myself getting closer and closer to the edge I begin to thrust back.

"Fill me with your cum!" I moan as I feel myself getting dangerously close.

A final thrust sends us both over the edge, I hear him grunt as he fills me with his cum, and I cry out as I climax.

# Chapter 6

A ndrew

Since that night in the hotel suite, Miss Lockmore and I have continued to make love and fuck. And not just on her fertile days.

*I think I'm really falling for her.*

As I sit down to check my last emails of the day, Sophie walks in. But she looks upset.

*Was it something I did? Did she find a new job?*

"Mr. Hayes I need to speak with you," she says without looking up.

"You know you can call me Andrew now, Sophie. Come and sit down," I gesture to the chair in front of the desk.

*Why won't she look at me?*

"Sophie, please tell me what's going on," I plead.

"Andrew I'm pregnant," she says with a sigh.

I can feel myself smiling.

*Pregnant! This is amazing! This woman is having my baby!*

*Why does she look so concerned? Does she not want the baby?*

I suddenly stop smiling.

*She doesn't want this, does she? I'll make it easy for her.*

"You don't have to keep it," I tell her.

Then she starts to cry.

*What did I do wrong?*

"I knew you wouldn't really want this," she sobs.

*Wait what? I do want this.*

"Sophie I do want this, but you seemed so concerned I didn't want to force you to do anything you weren't comfortable with," I say.

She looks up at me and doesn't say a word.

*What is she thinking?*

"Sophie I want us to be a family."

Her eyes get wide and the tears stop.

"A family? Not just an heir?" she questions.

"I want us to be a family. Unless you prefer something else?"

"I want us to be a family too! Andrew, I love you," she says quickly.

*Love? She loves me?*

*I think I love her, too. I've never felt this way about anyone, and knowing she's carrying my child just makes the feelings even stronger.*

"I will do anything I can to make you happy, I love you, too, Sophie".

# Chapter 7

**S**ophie

I can't believe how quickly your life can change in less than a year.

I step out of the elevator like I did the day we met, only this is my home now, too. I turn the corner and find Andrew sitting in one of the overstuffed chairs.

"Can I get you anything for lunch, Andrew?"

He looks up lovingly and smiles.

"No, Sophie Hayes, I'm just fine."

Ever since we made it official, he can't stop saying my new name. He gets up and places a hand on my growing belly.

"How is my son doing?" he asks.

That's another thing he loves saying these days...

"I love you, Andrew," I say as he smiles at my belly.

www.ingramcontent.com/pod-product-compliance
Lightning Source LLC
Chambersburg PA
CBHW052139150726

48002CB00006B/2678